The Lion

The Inner Circle Series #3

Kailin Gow

AUTHOR'S NOTE

Thank you for picking up The Lion, the third book in the Inner Circle Series.

This series is a New Adult Dark Romance and contains dark themes that may have some triggers. Recommended for 18+.

The Lion (The Inner Circle #3)

Summary

The 3rd Book in the Inner Circle Series...

The Inner Circle has sounded the alarm. Dante Black, aka, the Tin Man, one of our own Offspring Assassins of the Inner Circle's Founders, and the best has come back from the dead.

No longer a ghost, he has been taking us down one-by-one. Bent on revenge for what the Inner Circle did to him, his father, and that girl who he gave everything up for.

Now, according to Inner Circle rules, we are given the Go to bring him down.

I'm one of the Offsprings of the Inner Circle Founders, like the Tin Man. I'm known for my strength, my leadership abilities, and my charm. I'm the Lion, after all. We are all part of the surreal underground like Oz, only we are all ruthless, focused, and willing to do anything and everything to make the Inner Circle the organization what it is meant to be.

Now Dante Black, the blackest heart, and the man who literally had no heart, is my target.

Tin Man versus The Lion. It's Game On!

**The Inner Circle Series is a Dark College Romance Thriller with lots of action, steamy scenes, language, and twists and turns. Recommended for age 18 and up.

Prologue

<u>Dante Black/Thad Newton (formerly Parker James)</u>

Malibu, CA

Ace and I were back at my new Malibu ranch, listening in on a conversation at Rockefeller's office where we had planted a bug.

"It's my turn to go after that bastard Dante for you, Dad," a young man was saying. "The I.C. sent me word I have the sole privilege to take him down. I will, Dad or my name isn't Lion."

Ace turned to me and said, "So now, Lion's going to go after you. First Scarecrow and now Lion."

"It's to be expected," I said. "Inner Circle rules."

"What about Scarecrow?" Ace asked. "His trail went cold after he attempted to assassinate you at our old house."

"Guess he's out of the picture," I said. "One less Offspring to worry about."

"Hey, wait," Ace said. "I just got an update on news from my favorite personalities. Rob Raven's social media just went wild. Oh fuck! No way!"

"What, Ace? What's going on?" I asked walking up to him to look at his computer.

"Look! Ouch, that's bad," Ace said. "Rob Raven was found dead handcuffed to his bed after some wild bondage sex. He was also high. His mouth was full of powder." He shook his head. "I thought he was clean, but man, he was just like other rock stars."

I let Ace have a moment to grieve his favorite rocker before I said, "He probably was."

"Huh?" Ace asked. "He being on drugs would explain why he wasn't so good of an assassin as Scarecrow. He abandoned his mission after all."

So Ace already knew Rob Raven, the rock star was The Scare Crow. I didn't have to tell him.

"No, Ace," I said. "Someone from the I.C. took him out. Eliminated. Looks like someone really wanted to go after me for the kill instead of anyone else. And I think I know who it is."

"Are you going to take him out then?" Ace asked.

"No, but I know who I'm going to take down next in the Inner Circle. I think I'm going to play around with the minds of the Offsprings and the Founders a bit. It will make all my years of sacrifices worth it."

Chapter 1

<u>Thad Newton</u>
Malibu, CA

"Ace," I said, "how fast can you get the Broom ready?"

Ace laughed, "I can't believe you named your new Gulfstream 6200 the Broom."

"It's very Oz, isn't it?" I said. "Plus I couldn't name the Broom the same name I had for

Parker James' plane. Couldn't keep the LearJet after our cover was blown. Knowing how the Offsprings worked and that Dorothy knew Parker James' LearJet like the back of her hand since I took her on a couple of intimate trips to the Caribbean; I had to sell the LearJet."

"I know," Ace said. "I kinda liked Tornado. We've been to some interesting places riding on Tornado."

I grinned, "Yes, Tornado took us everywhere. I'll miss the Lear, but it's time to make some memories on the Broom."

Ace shook his head, "I can't complain. It sure beats flying commercial, even first class. Having your own jet is nothing less than what a billionaire whiz kid like Thad Newton would do. What Dante Black would do."

“Exactly,” I said. “Thad Newton is closer to being who I am than my previous cover Parker James.”

“But…” Ace said.

I put on my glasses, pushed aside my long copper-colored bangs that fell over one side of my face, and stood up from my comfortable leather armchair, knocking over the cocktail glass I had set on the table next to me. “Oh, my bad,” I guffawed like a nerd.

“Oh, okay,” Ace said shaking his head. “That right there. Nah, so *not* like Dante Black. He’s all cool, suave, deliberate, and you’re…”

“Not,” I said, standing straight up, assuming my confident Dante Black stance.

"You've got this new wimpy persona down," Ace said.

"Well, Thad Newton is opposed to violence, to punching anyone, and anything that may damage his glasses," I said.

Ace roared with laughter. "That is so *not* Dante Black, Boss."

"These macho guys and girls in the Inner Circle would never suspect Dante to be so wimpy… well, hopefully not," I said.

"But…" Ace said again.

"Thad is eccentric. He's a techno geek. A billionaire. The kid in high school who was the virgin nerd, picked on by the bullies, shunned by the cheerleaders. But when he went back to his high school reunion, he was the stud, the one who made it. So yes, Thad is going to be eccentric. He will be flashy. Not subtle like those born to wealth. Like pop stars, some reality tv stars, and even a few YouTubers, he will be putting on his newfound fame and wealth on full display."

"Like Megan Markle showing off her $14 million home in California on Oprah?" Ace said, "While still bemoaning how unprivileged she was."

"Unprivileged my foot," I said. "She's definitely more privileged than many people in this world. I don't know if she's just naïve or dense, but she basically just did a Marie Antoinette."

"Let them eat cake," Ace said. "Clueless how the poor were starving, lived in poverty; while she lived in a castle, showing off her trinkets, expensive dresses, and pampered pets. She threw lavish parties for her friends and threw away food and cakes like it didn't matter. Meanwhile the rest of her people starved, and were taxed to the point of poverty, just to support her spendthrift lifestyle."

"Led to the Revolution. People revolted. They were fed up," Ace continued.

"So, Marie Antoinette and her friends in high places who had taxed the middle class into poverty, and was now starving most of the people in their country; were executed. The people had enough!" I added.

"So, Thad," Ace said, "You'll be eccentric like that? An elitist?"

"No, I'll be eccentric in that I have the wealth of someone who can. Not fucking stupid like those who rub their wealth, which they don't really have or because their wealth is tied into taxing hard-working people's money that they are spending like it's unlimited. Thad Newton is eccentric in his own class because he's truly brilliant, bordering on crazy like Einstein. The Offsprings would recognize this in him, which would make them think twice about killing him. He's more useful to them alive than dead."

"Great cover, Boss. I can't wait to see what you have planned next," Ace said.

"So, pack your bag for a weekend trip, all your gears."

"Where are we heading?" Ace asked, "So I would know how to dress, you know."

"Switzerland," I said. "Let's see if Worth's secretary Anna would remember Parker James' cock."

Chapter 2

Thad Newton
Switzerland

"This is like deja vue, Boss," Ace said, walking into the luxury hotel, The Hotel Intercontinental Emerald, we last stayed in as Parker James.

"Our wonderful stay was cut short, Ace," I said. "Remember, we didn't get a chance to try out the restaurant next to this hotel."

"That's why we're here?" Ace asked.

"Of course," I smiled. "That and the fact I'm about to meet someone who might be a good ally for me. Not that he would know it."

"Okay, Boss," Ace said. "What do you want me to do besides the usual set up?"

"How would you like to step into my shoes for once?" I smiled.

"What?" Ace asked.

I went to my overnight bag and pulled out a smaller bag, tossing it to Ace, who caught it with both hands. He opened the zip and pulled out a black pair of pants, a black cap, and black jacket. He looked at the logo on the jacket and cap. "A to Z Teleco," he read.

I tossed him a box of hair dye. From my pocket, I took out a small contact lens case and handed it to him. Then I waited for it to sink in.

After Ace looked at the hair dye and the contacts, he grinned. "You want me to become Parker James?"

"Just look like him for a short time."

"But I don't look like you, Boss," Ace said. "I mean, I'm about an inch shorter, less filled-out, and…"

"I know. I know," I said. "Hence the disguise."

"Even with the outfit and the hair coloring," Ace said, "I'm not going to pass for being you."

I took out another bag and said, "Hollywood magic, Kid. By the time I'm finished with you, everyone will think you are Parker James."

*****

Observing from the hotel penthouse suite's window with a high-powered binocular a couple of hours later, I watched Ace walked out of the hotel, dressed in the jacket, cap, and pants Parker James wore when he entered the Worth Financials building last time. His hair was a nice platinum silver under the cap a la Parker James, and he sported a black mask over his nose and mouth.

I watched him walk right over to the Worth Financial building near the hotel and go through the doors. "Good job, Kid," I spoke out loud to myself. Ace made it through security without anyone stopping him at the door. The next step was for him to make it through the metal detectors before entering the rest of the building.

I waited with a bit of nervousness. It was Ace's first time impersonating me as Parker James. A thief and hacker background made him very good as my assistant, but could he pull off having to be like me when I needed him to?

Moments later, I saw the signal in the window. The curtains were drawn opened. It was well worth the ten thousand dollars per night that I had paid for the penthouse suite to get this view. And it was definitely Thad Newton's style to stay in the best room. Yes, the view of Worth's office was definitely worth this luxury suite. Ace was in Worth's office itself, and he had either pulled the curtains of the office's windows opened himself or gotten Anna Guther, the lovely and hyper-horny secretary of Worth to do it for him. Either way, the opening of the window's curtains was the signal.

And for sure, the sounds I was hearing in Worth's office meant that Ace was in the hole. Or, the other way. Ace had managed to plant a bug in the office, like I had before, as Parker James.

I heard the sound of a zipper being unzipped, then some sucking noises, gulping, and panting. "Oh yeah," Ace's voice sounded constrained.

"How's it going?" I said into my mic.

"Very good," Ace could barely talk. His voice had gotten hoarse.

Then a woman's squeal. Anna's. "Oh I must be pleasing you immensely," she said. "You're bigger than last time you came to fix the internet problem. You were immense before but today, you're absolutely huge. My mouth adore you."

"My cock adore you, Anna," Ace said. "It'll adore you even more when you keep going." He was groaning. "Yes, that's it. You're very talented, Anna."

"Yes, one of many talents I have, Parker," she said.

"You'll be much better if you concentrate more on squeezing, sucking…oh yeah, that's it," Ace was groaning again. "Yes, oh yes, fuck. I'm coming!"

I heard a deep groan, and then Anna's lips smacking.

I shook my head and chuckled. Who knew Ace was hung like a horse. I certainly didn't. He apparently wasn't a virgin either, which I knew. He was a good-looking young guy. I was sure he knew his way around a woman's pussy. Well, I promised he could have a shot with the lusty secretary from Switzerland, if she was interested so I guessed he did. Spectacularly, too.

I walked quickly out the suite, headed for Worth Financials. I made it through the front door, but as I pass through the metal detectors, there was a beep.

"Sir, can you empty your pockets?" the guard asked.

"Sure," I said, unloading my pockets into a tray.

"What about your briefcase?" the guard asked.

"I can't let my briefcase through," I said.

"No?" the guard asked. "Sir, you have to in order to come into the building."

"You see, I can't," I said, indicating the handcuff I had on my right wrist chained to the briefcase with another.

"Then you will have to leave, sir," the guard said. "We can't let you in."

"But what will I say to Mr. Worth when he finds out I couldn't make my appointment with him to discuss where I should invest my money?" I indicated my briefcase.

The guard looked surprised. "You're one of Mr. Worth's clients?"

"Well, I wouldn't trust my billions to just anyone," I said.

"Wait, hold on," another voice said, walking up to the guard and me. It was Wellington Worth, Mr. Worth's son. Handsome in an arrogant and cold way, with black hair and blue eyes, he reminded me of how I used to be as Dante Black. Although we have never met, I knew of him.

Almost anyone who had kept up with stocks, finances, and the world economy would have heard of him. A chip off the old block, like his father, Wellington was a financial genius. A wizard of wealth and numbers. At just 22 years old, he was the youngest funds manager of the biggest funds in all of Europe.

"Thad Newton, isn't it?" Wellington asked.

"Yes," I said. "How do you know?"

"I read about you acquiring all kinds of businesses here and there, including Parker James' security company as well as Black Biotech," Wellington said.

"Yes, that was something I couldn't pass up," I said. "Building my portfolio, you see."

"Good to diversify," Wellington said. He looked at me with a glint in his eyes and a smile. "So you are here visiting Switzerland on business?"

"Well, I was just thinking of doing some skiing, getting some sightseeing, getting some Swiss chocolates for a girl I'm really into. And of course I have to do some shopping."

"So you're here for pleasure," Wellington said.

"Yes, but I might as well do some business, too," I said. "I'm Thad Newton so of course I'm always thinking of business. So while I'm here in Switzerland, why not see what Worth Financials is about."

"So you're thinking of becoming a client?" Wellington asked.

"Possibly," I said.

Wellington waved at the guards to let me through the metal detector, and came up close to me to talk to me. "Well, come on in. At Worth Financials, we always welcome billionaires like yourself, Mr. Newton."

"I see," I said. "It takes one to know one."

Wellington smiled charmingly. "Looks like we have some things in common."

I laughed, "I'll say."

Chapter 3

Wellington Worth

What luck.

Here was the billionaire boy wonder himself. Thad Newton.

Walking through the security checks of my own building, with a silver briefcase handcuffed to his own wrist. Every article I could find on him painted him as an eccentric. But I didn't think he himself would walk in like that.

It was bold and brash.

Something this guy walking next to me with a bit of a clumsy gait and emo wimpy mannerisms didn't seem capable of. He walked through the security check confidently, but when he began walking alongside me, his entire body soften into an insecure geek nerd shuffle.

"Mr. Newton," I said, "You are a very private person. I usually have a good pulse on all the movers and shakers out there in the world of finance and business, so I was able to learn a little about you."

"Oh," Thad said, coughing and then pushing up his glasses that fell down his nose as he coughed. He took out a handkerchief and sneezed into it, wheezing a little as he did.

I couldn't help but move a little away as he coughed, wheeze, and sneeze. Disgusting. I hated germs. I, myself, have always tried to avoid them as much as I could.

Which meant I asked my staff at the Worth Financial building to wipe down surfaces every hour or so. For people who came into our building who we contracted with like service providers, they knew about our mask policies. They should wear them to not spread their germs around the areas I would frequent.

Those contractors who knew about my policies often found their contracts extended. But I couldn't require the same stringent rules to a client. Damn.

"Are you feeling alright?" I asked Thad.

"Oh, yes," he said taking another handkerchief and blowing into it. "I think I caught a cold. Thought it was warmer on the slopes so I just wore a short-sleeve t-shirt under my jacket. Was freezing the entire time." He sneezed again. Without catching his sneeze with a handkerchief. I tried not to breathe as I watch the mist of germ pellets flying all over me.

So disgusting.

My phone rang, and I took that opportunity to step away, walking far enough to have some distance from that walking snot slobbering machine.

"Wellington," my father said. "The Lion is on the prowl. He tried to trace Parker James' whereabouts, but found he had disappeared. Vanished. The Lion sent a warning to everyone in the I.C. that he thinks Parker James has taken another identity."

"Does he have any idea who he had morphed into?" I asked.

"His biggest guess would be the person who bought his company. A Tad Newsom," Dad said.

"You mean Thad Newton," I corrected. I wiped my face with a sanitizer wipe and tossed it away into a trash can nearby.

"Yes, that's it," Dad said.

"Why him?" I asked.

"He said that Parker James' company's passwords and system infrastructure didn't change at all since Newton took over. That was suspicious."

I nodded. “Lion’s pretty good about hacking into a company’s systems and checking things out like that,” I said. “I will keep a close eye on Newton.”

I looked over at Thad, who was standing where I left him. He was looking into his phone. Yes, I’d keep a close eye on him alright.

“Hey Dad,” I said, “I’ve got a potential new client with me. You wouldn’t guess who it is.”

“Well, whoever it is, reel him in,” Dad said.

My phone rang, “Dad, I have another call coming in. I’ll talk to you later?”

“Sure. Go ahead and do your work,” Dad said. “You’re the future of Worth Financials, Son. Heck, you’re the future of the I.C. Now that Clay,

Stan, and Rockefeller's gone…not to mention Rob "The Scare Crow"… there's only a few of us Founders of the I.C. left along with their Offsprings."

"Outlast the others, and we're going to be the one taking it all, aren't we, Dad?" I asked.

"That's the plan, Son," Dad said. "But Dante Black? He's the loose end. He should have died. But he didn't. Now we have to make sure he does."

"Lion's on his tail," I said. "And Dorothy's inching to get at him, too. I'll let them handle him."

"Dante Black is the real deal, Son," Dad said. "He's the Assassin amongst assassins. That was his sole role in the I.C. You and the rest of the Offsprings like Lion, Scare Crow, and Dorothy only think you're real assassins, but you all have other jobs besides that. Dante Black, well, he's a league of his own. We sent him to do all our dirty jobs since he was a kid. It's what he knows."

I gulped. "Dante Black is that good? That dangerous?"

"Yes, Son," Dad said. "His father raised him to be as cold-hearted as possible. Even took out his beating human heart through a so-called car accident that resulted in a heart surgery. Replaced it with a mechanical one. His father Clay was the most ruthless son-of-a-bitch I've ever known, and Dante is said to be even worst since he literally is heartless."

"So, Lion thinks Dante is now Thad Newton?" I asked, looking at Thad with scrutinizing eyes.

"Yes," Dad said. "Lion has good reasons to believe Thad Newton is Dante Black. Lion is looking everywhere for Thad Newton now. He found out Thad owned a private jet which took off to Switzerland hours ago. He should be arriving here soon. Switzerland is our playground, Son, that means we'll have an upper hand if he's here. But if he's here, that also means, he's here for a reason."

"To take you out, Dad," I said.

"Yes," he said. "I'm next on his list. Of all the Founders, it's just me and Claire left to take out."

"I won't let him take you out, Dad," I said. "I'll kill him before he even steps into your office."

"That's my boy," Dad said. "That's why I can trust you with running Worth Financials.

That's why I can trust you in running the I.C. eventually, because let's face it. Claire and her Offspring Dorothy certainly couldn't. Dorothy's a demented and deranged lunatic, and Claire…well, you know where Dorothy gets that from."

I looked at my phone. My other caller had hung up and sent me a text message instead. Head of Security at the Worth Financials building.

HOS: Parker James is on the premise.

My eyes barely registered my surprise. So, Thad Newton really *is* Parker James.

"Hey Dad," I said, still on the phone with him. "Talk of the Devil. Dante Black aka Parker James is here in the building. He was spotted."

"Oh, that's not good," Dad said.

"Don't worry," I said. "I don't think he knows we're onto him. And I think I know where he is. I'll take him out before he even knows it. See you later."

"Be careful, Son," Dad said.

"Don't worry," I said. "Dante Black looks like he's lost his physique. Sick. Under-the-weather. Now's the best time to strike."

"I'll call in security," Dad said.

"You don't even have to do that," I said. "It looks like it'll be a piece of cake."

"Well, you are a martial artist," Dad said. "And you're smart. Just don't be too cocky."

"Don't worry, Dad," I said. "I've got this. Soon the world will be rid of Dante Black once and for all. Gotta get to work. Bye."

Chapter 4

Thad Newton

"Did you hear that conversation?" Ace asked.

"Yes," I said into my micro-sized microphone. Ace and I had synced up into the bug he placed in Worth's office so we both could hear what was going on within Worth's office, while still able to communicate with each other. "So they think Dante Black is Parker James, and Parker James is Thad."

"Boss, what should we do?" Ace asked.

"Stay in the building. Make sure you're seen in the security cameras. If it get close, and they corner you, fight your way out, as I've taught you," I said. "I know your location. I'll find you. But if I don't, move on to the next step without me. Carry on the mission."

Ace gulped. "Okay, I'll do my best."

"You're doing great," I said. "Just play it cool. You're Parker James now. You know what to do."

"Okay, yeah, I'm Parker James," Ace repeated, doubtfully.

"Remember your own mission," I said. Ace had personally been burned by the Inner Circle to the point where he lost everything. When I found him, he was running away from the cartel and almost beaten to death. Fighting my way through the cartel and saving his life made him forever grateful and loyal, but it was the mission we both shared…the mission to bring down the Inner Circle for what they have done to us personally, was what made us dead set on completing the mission.

“Ace?” I asked when I didn’t hear back from him.

“Gotta go,” he said, “Anna’s leading me to the internet room.” I heard him call out to Anna, who seemed to be an earshot away. “I’m coming.”

“Yes, you will,” Anna giggled. “We’ll have more privacy in the internet room. Cool dark place with just data boxes and wires. No one there to disturb us. Too bad Mr. Worth showed up from his lunch break too early. Back at his office.”

"Lucky you," I said laughing.

Ace chuckled back. "Good to be you," he said.

I sneaked a peek over at Wellington while I fixed my cuffs. One of the cufflinks held a tiny amount of pepper concoction that I needed in order to cause quite a commotion.

Suddenly, I heard Ace saying out loud as if he was talking to Anna, "Hey, a bunch of men just showed up. Are they supposed to?"

"Get them," I said, as Wellington reached me, like he didn't just have a call with his father about killing me. "I've just been asked to the dance, too. Show time."

Ace didn't answer, but I could hear him ask, "So where do you hide from the sex police?" right as I turned to face Wellington with an explosive sneeze that made me blow the liquid pepper mix I had been inhaling which made me sneeze and cough all day…right into his face. Bulls-eye.

"Holy…" Wellington bellowed, taking out his handkerchief and wiping his face repeatedly. "It's gotten into my eyes. My eyes. Your germs!"

"Hey, man," I said, "I'm so," I coughed harder on him, spitting more of the pepper fumes into his nostrils until he was sneezing. "Sorry," I took out my used handkerchief and tried wiping down the front of his shirt, managing to place a clear and almost invisible bug into his shirt's front pocket.

"Don't breathe on me," Wellington cried out. "Oh God, how disgusting. I've never," he began coughing.

"Sorry, man," I said again, coughing up a storm.

Wellington managed to pull out a sanitizer wipe and had wiped his nose with it, removing the pepper mix I had sprayed on him. He was beginning to stop coughing and sneezing. But his eyes were tearing up.

"Hey, I didn't mean to spread my germs on you," I said, "but I couldn't help it. Been sickly since I was a child. Smallest kid in the orphanage. Couldn't play any sports so I tinkered with electronics instead. Total nerd."

"Whatever you caught, it's potent," Wellington said. He dabbed his eyes dry and said,

"Luckily, I've always had a strong disposition. Good immune system. I think I got out whatever it was at its initial stage. Whew!" he let out a breath. "I feel much better now."

He reached into his pockets to take out a silver pill box with an engraved "W" on its cover. "W" for Wellington. "W" for Worth. And now I know for sure. "W" for the Wizard, code name for Worth's Offspring. And one of the I.C. assassins who was sent to go after me.

Wellington took out a pill and popped it in his mouth. "Special pill. Great for increasing my strength, stamina, and immunity. Made by LaFleur Industries. They're a food company specializing in natural and organic foods but now make supplements and health products. Maybe they will be a good investment for you. They're like Black Biotech, which you own."

I shook my head. “Then why would I want to own their stocks? I already have Black Biotech.”

“They’re aggressively growing. One of the fastest conglomerate that has grown in the last couple of years. They’re set on becoming a major global player in the Black Biotech space. And their supplements are amazing! I recommend it for the onset of any colds or flu.”

“No,” I shook my head. “I’ll be fine. I always catch colds and the flu every season. I know what to expect. How I’ll react. I’m used to it.”

“Sure,” Wellington said. “Your choice. Your body.”

“Yes, that’s what I believe, too, dude,” I said laughing.

I looked at him closely. For an Offspring, he was probably the most compatible to Thad Newton. Brainiac. Into numbers. Into finance. Manic, compulsive.

Wellington smiled charmingly. "Now that we both stopped sneezing, shall we proceed to my office where we can do business?"

"Yes, sure," I said.

He led the way to the elevators, and I walked in with him.

When the doors closed, I saw him shift his position into an offensive pose. He was getting ready to strike. It was a subtle shift, but to the trained eye like mine, I knew he was no longer the charming financial manager, but had shifted into I.C. mode to become The Wizard. The elevator was speeding to the top, but he managed to stopped the elevator, pushing the emergency button, which made the elevator jump, halting it like a speeding train stopping in its track. Wellington jumped into the air and came at me like a ninja, whacking me on the nose with his elbow.

I felt my head fly back like a whiplash. "Fucking Owww, man!" I yelled out. "What the fuck?"

I braced myself from crumbling to the ground. With my free hand, I wiped my nose. It was wet. I knew it was from my blood. I was bleeding. Resisting the urge to throttle The Wizard's neck, I winced in pain, whining how much it hurt.

Wellington's eyes were like a cobra's. Focused and deadly. "I can't believe that's all you've got," he said.

"What the fuck are you talking about?" I asked pathetically. "Are you trying to pick a fight with me? What the fuck? Is this how you treat a potential client?"

"You're not here to become our client," Wellington said. "We're on to you, Parker James."

"Who?" I asked, bewildered. "Are you crazy? How the fuck did you get from me being Parker James? I'm Thad Newton. Thad Newton."

Wellington laughed. "Yeah, that's what you want us to think, Parker. You're still Parker. You didn't change anything when you bought your own company, Thad. You think we're a bunch of idiots?"

"No, you've got me all wrong," I said. "My team's working on changing the security system there, but it takes time. But now that I know you had someone hack into my company's security, testing the passwords, I'll let them know to beef up the security." I narrowed my eyes at him angrily. "Fucktard. Not only did you beat me up but, you got everything wrong. I heard Parker James' all tough, strong, athletic. Big bodybuilder physique. Me, I only wish I was half his size."

Without warning, Wellington's fist went crashing into my chest. I didn't even try to block it, but fell back into the elevator wall, collapsing to the ground. My eyes closed and my mouth fell open.

"Fuck!" Wellington said, "Why is it that easy? Fight back."

I remained crumpled on the ground, my face blank, my eyes closed, my mouth open like a dead fish.

“Something’s off,” Wellington said to himself. “It can’t be that easy to take down Dante Black.” A phone began ringing, and Wellington took his phone out of his pocket. “Hey, what’s going on?”

I remained like a dead fish.

“Oh fuck! It can’t be. Parker James was spotted in the internet control room? When? A few minutes ago?” He kicked the side of the elevator hard. “Fuck! He escaped? You sure, he was Parker James? My father’s secretary Anna confirmed it. She had his business card? Fucking unbelievable!”

I felt his angry eyes staring at me as he slammed another foot into the wall.

A minute later, I felt his hands lifting me to my feet. "Hey listen, Mr. Newton. About what happened just now. I apologize. It's those pills. They make me act strange. Yeah, that's it. Mr. Newton? Are you alright?"

I felt a slight slapping on my cheeks. I finally opened my eyes with a groan. "My nose," I whined. "I think it's broken."

"Don't worry. I have a really good doctor. We can get you fix up nice and new," Wellington said. He pulled out his phone and asked for a doctor. After his call ended, he wiped my bloody nose with his sanitizer wipe and said, "I hope you don't think Worth Financials any less than you did because of my inexcusable behavior towards you just now."

“You attacked me,” I winced. “What was that about?’

“I went a little nuts. The pills. The sneezing. I thought you were someone else, and I got confused,” Wellington tried to explain his attempt to kill me, away.

I shuddered, moving away from him. “I don’t know if I want someone like you to handle my money,” I said. “I want someone reliable. Stable. Level-headed. Not someone who flies off the handle like you did.”

“Again, I apologize Mr. Newton,” Wellington said. He pressed the button for the elevator to proceed, and we started going up. “I don’t know what got into me. Normally we are not like this at all. Worth Financials offers the most top-notch service of our clients. If you can’t trust me to be stable and level-headed… at least trust my father, Mr. Henrich Worth, himself. He will be the one managing your portfolio for you. He's brilliant and have made several of his clients wealthier than they can ever dream. Just give us a chance."

I sucked in a shaky breath and shuddered. "I've never been attacked so badly before. Let alone by someone who wanted my business. I can't stand disrespect like that. Clients comes first to me. That's how I became so successful. I expect every vendor and service provider who I hire to have that same philosophy."

"We do," Wellington said. "Again, I apologize profusely. I am really sorry." He was wringing his hands.

"Okay, since we seem to have a lot in common, and I thought you were a decent guy before you attacked me," I said. "I'll meet your father."

Wellington sighed. "Sure. That's where we're headed now. To his office."

Chapter 5

Thad Newton

Henrich Worth was just as overbearing in person as he was on our hidden camera when I last saw him fucking his lusty secretary Anna. He was seated at his desk when I was led in by Wellington.

"My God," he exclaimed looking at my bloodied face, messed up hair, and crumpled clothes. "What happened to you?"

I looked over angrily at Wellington. Worth didn't miss that look and narrowed his eyes at his son. He got up and walked over to me, putting his hand on my shoulder. "I apologize for the mistreatment you've had if whatever happened to you happened on our premises."

"It more than happened on your premise," I said. "Your son, here, attacked me. Broke my nose. Just went flat out crazy on me. I question his mental capacity and stability."

Worth shook his head. "I'm sorry for all of this. Is there anything I can do to assuage your mishandling?"

"Mishandling? A broken nose? Being punched to the point I almost died. And I was already so sick to begin with. Is this how you treat a visitor to your country? Is this how you treat a potential big client?" I was angry. "Your son almost killed me for no reason at all, except he took some medication that made him so beserk." I clutched my hands to my chest and huddled over. "I've never been so scared in my life."

"I'm sorry, again," Worth said. "I can't excuse my son for such bad behavior. The only thing I can do is fire him. He may be my son, but I can't have behavior like that in my organization. Clients come first to us at Worth Financials." He looked over at Wellington and said, "You have no excuse for how you treated Mr…."

"Newton," I said.

Worth's eyebrows went up in surprise. "Newton? As in Thad Newton?"

"The one and only," I said.

"Dad," Wellington said. "I can explain. I thought Mr. Newton here was someone else. A Parker James, but apparently he wasn't as the real

Parker James was found by our security in the Internet central room."

"Oh, that is surprising," Worth said. "So…Mr. Newton is really just Mr. Newton. I mean, he is not just, but he is the one and only Mr. Thad Newton, whom we would love to be doing business with."

"Yes, Dad," Wellington said.

"Please excuse my son's stupidity and misbehavior," Worth said. "I always said, 'don't do drugs' because it messes with your mind, but you know how they are. They never listen. Again, I will fire him from our company if it makes you feel uncomfortable that he is here. Whatever we can do to make you trust us again."

I looked at Wellington, who looked like he wanted to cry. His entire life seemed to be tied into his family business. "Look, I don't want to get him out of his family business," I said. "I don't want you to fire him. But you should know his attack on me is unacceptable. I could have died. I could have him arrested."

"Tell me what I can do to make it right," Worth said. He looked genuinely worried now.

I sat down in the plush armchair across from his desk and said. "Okay, let's talk."

Chapter 6

Thad Newton

"Damn," Ace said. "I couldn't believe you just walked into Worth's office like that while I barely escaped with my life."

"For now," I said changing out of my Thad Newton outfit. I removed my fake layer of fat around my stomach, which had made it easy for me to stoop over and looked a little out of shape as the nerdy emo and sickly Thad Newton.

I sank down into the luxurious sofa in the hotel's penthouse suite. Although Wellington had called his doctor to check me out at Worth's office, I refused the medical care, careful not to expose the prosthetics I wore to shape me into another person. Luckily, the extra cushioning on my chest and stomach helped deflected Wellington's punch to my chest. I knew it would hurt, and I would have to take it. Even if I had to break my nose, I had to go through with acting helpless and defenseless.

In the end, it was worth it. I've convinced Worth and his Offspring The Wizard that I was not Dante Black, but Thad Newton. And now as Thad Newton, I was their number one client with the potential of ruining them.

"It wasn't so bad, wasn't it?" I said, nursing my nose with a bag of ice. "You got to meet Anna's talented mouth, didn't you?"

Ace laughed. "Yeah, the one chance to live in your shoes as Parker James, was totally worth it, You get the thrills with the danger. Anna completely thought I was you. Welcomed me into the building with a smile, walking with me through another entrance to bypass the metal detector and straight up to Worth's office. Where she proceeded to give my dick a hearty and enthusiastic welcome."

"So I heard," I said drily.

"Yeah, I nearly forgot you could hear everything going on, but when in the moment... boy, I'm in love," Ace sighed.

"You barely escaped, though," I said. "How did you?"

“I saw a number of men entering the room where Anna had led me to after her big BJ, and well, she continued another round there, too,” Ace gulped. “Yeah, she’s good.”

“The story?” I said. “What happened?”

“Well, the men in black were beginning to walk in one by one while Anna was still sucking my dick. The leader recognized her, stopped moving forward, and waved the men out. I guess he didn’t want to get in trouble with Anna since she was Worth’s personal secretary. Probably the one who orders them around, too. They walked out, leaving Anna and me alone. After I came, I asked where was a discrete way to get out, and she pointed to the floor. Yeah, so I high-tailed it out of there using their tunnels right as Anna walked out of the room.”

I laughed, "Excellent escape plan, Ace. You got the girl, and you got away." I looked him over and said, "That silver platinum look of Parker James do suit you."

Ace looked surprised. "It does? I was going to change my hair back to black."

"No, I'll need you to play Parker for a little longer."

"Why?" Ace asked.

I looked at my watch and said, "Because the Lion has just landed in Switzerland."

Chapter 7

Wellington/The Wizard

I walked out of Dad's office with a big bruise on my eye. I counted myself lucky that was the only bruise I had.

Dad was fucking furious.

"What the hell happened?" he bellowed as soon as Thad Newton walked out of Dad's office, leaving Dad and me alone. I had offered to accompany Thad out, but he didn't want me near him. He didn't want me alone with him. It was lucky he didn't press charges against me and file a lawsuit against Worth Financials.

"I thought he was Dante," I said. "I was ready to kill him."

"But…" Dad said, his eyes like flames. I've never seen him this mad before.

"He wasn't Dante, but Thad Newton, who has a portfolio as diverse and stellar as I've never seen. You've seen the sheet I text over. For a kid still in his early 20s, he's amassed a potential net worth that Branson, Musk, and even Bezos would be jealous of. By the time he's their age at the rate he's going, he would surpass them."

Dad swung his fist into my eye, knocking me back hard onto the ground. "So you fucking screw it up," he roared. "We haven't had someone with that kind of potential walk in here for decades. Hell, ever. This is a once in a lifetime opportunity, and you. Fucking. Screwed. It. Up."

He took out a pistol and pointed it at me. “I should just kill you now. I’m ashamed to have such a screw-up for a son. I’m better off without a son at all.”

“Dad!” I pleaded. “I was just following orders. You said Lion said Thad Newton was Parker James, and that Parker James was Dante Black. I was just trying to take out Dante Black before he could get to you.”

Dad had walked around his desk to point his pistol at my forehead point blank. From the steel gaze of his eyes, I knew he was serious about killing me. He was a Founder of the Inner Circle after all.

“Dad! Dad!” I cried, tears running down my cheeks. “Please! Give me another chance. I won’t screw up. Please!”

Dad hesitated.

"I'm your only child! Dad! Your legacy. Who's going to take over your company and keep your legacy alive but me? Dad!"

His gun was still pointed at me when his phone rang. With one hand, he picked it up and said, "What's up?"

His face contorted into annoyance and he let out a loud, "Fuck. Are you kidding me? What's with these Offsprings going rogue? Claire, you get your kid in line, and I'll handle mine. And Rockefeller's son… the plans have changed."

I waited with bated breath to see if Dad was going to go through with killing me.

Finally, he stood up straight and withdrew his pistol. "Son," he said. "You've been redeemed. You get to live."

I let out a deep breath before crumbling to the floor, my entire body relieved.

"Get off the ground and stop crying," Dad said. "I didn't raise my kid to be a fucking wimp."

I immediately got up and brushed myself off.

"Here," Dad said, handing me his gun. "Lion just landed in Switzerland, and he's heading over here. Says he's after Dante Black." He looked me square in the eyes and said, "I know he's doing I.C. business, but I don't want him messing with Worth Financials' business too. We are loyal to the I.C., but I didn't spend my entire life building up

Worth Financials from the business your great grandfather started years ago for nothing."

"So what do you want me to do, Dad?" I said, getting focused and back to business.

"The Lion gave us wrong information. Unsubstantiated intel. Did he have a bias against Thad Newton that would make him pinpoint him as Parker James? We can't go with bias reporting. It's not truthful, honest, and reliable. We go with substantiated evidence. Evidence that is logical and makes sense. That's how companies that want to thrive and survive make their decisions. Got that? If you want Worth Financials to survive. Heck if you want countries to survive and thrive, leaders need to make smart and wise decisions based on substantiated real facts and evidence, not biased reports. Lion should've known better. He just took over Rockefeller Real Estate Assets. He can't go making speedy dumb assumptions like that. What we do here at the Inner Circle is run the key industries in the world. What we do affect trillions of people. That so-called supplement you took that made you act so crazy…was it from LaFleur Industries? Claire and her companies are horrendous and horrible. Looks like there's a defect in her supplements, but she doesn't seem to care. That needs to be addressed too. Her work is going to be the end of the I.C. We have standards, and she is not measuring up."

"Yes, Dad," I said, awaiting his orders.

"I want you to deal with Lion and his mistake. It nearly got the wrong man killed. For that, I almost killed you for it."

I nodded. Without having to say it, I knew what Dad wanted me to do. It was the Assassin's way. It was the Inner Circle way.

Chapter 8

Thad Newton

"The Lion has landed," I said to Ace in our penthouse suite while I looked out our 180 degree windows down to the street below. Using my high-powered binoculars I could see a large lion-of-man about my age, getting out of a taxi, wearing a tan custom suit that nearly matched his long full mane of wild rock star hair. "He even looks like a lion," I chuckled. "How ironic."

"Really?" Ace asked, coming over.

"Here, take a look," I handed him my binoculars.

"You are not kidding. Wow, everything about him shouts, 'I'm Lion," Ace said.

"Get this," I had to shake my head. "His real name is Leo, as in 'lion'. He's Leo Rockefeller, the new President and CEO of Rockefeller Real Assets. He was named CEO of it by the Board, right after his father died."

"So he's the Offspring now on your trail," Ace said.

"Yes, and the one who still thinks Thad Newton is Dante Black," I said.

Ace handed me the binoculars, looking scared. "He's a big guy. Even bigger than you are, Boss. Shouldn't we be packing up and jetting off somewhere far away from him about now?"

"Repeat our last stay in Switzerland the same way as in when we were running out of this very same hotel from a murdering Summer, who was actually Kathryn or Dorothy?" I asked. "No, can't do that again. We haven't even had the chance to try that restaurant with authentic Swiss food next to the hotel."

"But he's making his way here," Ace said.

I handed him the binoculars and said, "Look again."

Ace looked through the binoculars and was now following along with the Lion below. "You're right. He walked past the hotel and straight towards Worth Financials."

Ace handed me the binoculars. "Why?"

I crossed my arms and leaned up against the wall. "Turn on the bugs we've planted in Worth's office and on the Wizard. We sure wouldn't want to miss this."

Chapter 9

The Lion

As soon as I walked through the doors of Worth Financials, I knew I made a mistake.

I was 'welcomed' by a swarm of men in black. You'd think I was some science fiction alien invading Earth. Yeah, I was a diehard science fiction freak like that. Rather, I was a film freak.

That was my passion. It's my favorite escape since I lived in such a hustle bustle world of real estate assets. New York real estate, but really, my company Rockefeller Real Estate Asset was global.

"Hey guys," I said looking at them. "So, where's Tommy Lee Jones?"

I heard a dry laugh and looked over to my right. It's been a few years since I've seen him in person, but I would recognize the Wizard anywhere. He and I were opposites in looks. Where he had dark hair, I had blonde. Where I was big and bulky muscular, he was thin and wiry. Where he was European genteel, I was New York.

"Hey Well," I called out. "How are you doing?"

"Leo," Wellington said, "You're looking big. Who knew you'd grow into a giant?"

"And your English," I said. "It's improved."

“I see yours has, too,” Wellington said.

“Funny,” I cracked a small smile and looked around at the men around me. Around five of them. All dressed like they were some secret service agents. Come on. At least dress like something high tech, futuristic. They’re Swiss after all, weren’t they? Originators of the Swiss clocks, Swiss army knives, and Swiss cheese. Really technical people. “You have some sense of humor.”

“I see you like tan,” Wellington said, looking at my suit.

“The better for me to blend in…not,” I said. “Hey I know you and your father’s happy to see me, but this…wow, what a welcome party.”

"Glad you showed up," Wellington said. "We have some things planned for you."

I looked at the five men in black around me and said, "If you must know, I swing another way."

Wellington actually laughed. "You and your jokes, man," he said, reminding me of the skinny kid from Switzerland who joined me, Scare Crow, and Dorothy at some summer camp where we learned how to do combat fighting, use weapons, think strategically… basically assassin training camp that our parents had set up for us out of jealousy, knowing how Dante Black, the only Offspring who was the same age as we were, but already a pro. And we sucked.

"Yeah, good times," I said.

“I still remembered you swallowing all that water when we had to go through the water coffin test,” Wellington said. “I was just thinking even the big guy couldn’t handle it. That made me feel better.”

“I’m sure it did,” I said. “I think I swallowed almost a pint that day. Quenched my thirst.”

“I’d say you were going with the ‘flow’,” Wellington said, almost laughing at his own corny joke.

I shook my head. Still the financial nerd genius. Annoying. On the other hand, he was the smartest of all the Offsprings so that wasn’t bad. You’d want him on your team. Fighting skills? He was also top-notched. Since he had trained in martial arts religiously, he was fast, strong, and accurate.

Me? I rely a lot on brute strength. And masculinity. If I wasn't in real estate, I'd be a lumberjack. My punch is like being hit with a sledgehammer. As far as my skills? I studied kickboxing, but can handle any firearms. Heck, I lived in New York, and walked to work from my penthouse nearby, let any would-be mugger be damn if he or she tried to mess with me. I hate driving and avoid it as much as I could. Hence I like my walks. I didn't even bother renting a car on this trip, opting to get a taxi instead. How's that for an assassin? I don't even have my own transport out of a I.C. job if I had it. It's been a long while since I did have an I.C. job, which made me a bit rusty. So when I could, I would joke.

"Dude, your jokes are killer," I said. "You should come visit me in New York. I'll hook you up with some of our finest comedy clubs there and get you started on a career as a stand up."

“Now you’re being the funny one,” Wellington said.

“So, old friend,” I said. “How’s the cocktails here?”

Wellington smiled and said, “Killer.”

“For old times’ sakes,” I said. “I’d like to have one before we get started with business.”

Wellington looked like he was mulling my suggestion over for a second. Then he looked at his squad of men in black, gave them a nod, and the leader waved them away while disappearing with them into some dark corner where they crawled from. Like spiders.

Wellington waved me through the metal detector and came over to put his arm around my shoulder. “Welcome to Worth Financials, Leo.”

As soon as he called me by my real name Leo, I knew we were no longer in I.C. mode. We were friends again going way back. "Remember that time when you were celebrating your 21st birthday and flew out to New York?" I said. "We bumped into each other in a club."

"Club 85," Wellington said. "Fucking wild night."

"Yeah, it sure was," I said. "Would never forget it. Although, there were some parts that I did forget."

"How could you not remember all of it?" Wellington said. "It was crazy."

"That's probably why I would have forgotten some parts of it, conveniently."

“It wouldn’t be the part where we somehow found ourselves locked in a room together?” Wellington asked.

“Coincidentally?” I said. “Maybe not. But what are the chances that two Offsprings from the I.C. would end up at the same club that night, locked in a room together.”

“Then there were those hot babes, fully nude,” Wellington said.

“Yeah, they were all over us, ripping our clothes off, sucking on our dicks, wrapping themselves around us,” I said.

“Under any other circumstance, I would be enjoying what they were doing,” Wellington said.

"Under any circumstance, I did," I said. "I think I fucked every one of them twice at some point or even five times. I lost count."

"They were insatiable," Wellington said. "I think I fucked every one of them twice, too. I lost count."

"I know. I think they were trying to kill us," I said. "Death by fucking."

Wellington roared with laughter. "You know, I think you're right."

"What the fuck," I said. "I think that was it. Because the next morning when we emerged out of the room, still breathing with our dicks intact, a bit drunk and woozy, the owner of the club looked at us like he couldn't believe we were still alive."

"Still able to walk," Wellington said.

“That was when he pulled a shotgun at us,” I said.

“I was completely unprepared,” Wellington said. “Luckily, you had your wits about you, even after an entire night and morning of fucking.”

“Yeah, it was just instinctual or habitual. I’m from New York, you know. It’s my own neighborhood,” I said. “I pulled out my own gun and shot him right there.”

Wellington looked at me in all seriousness, “You grabbed me and hauled me out of the club,” he said. “Saved my ass for another day.”

“What can I say,” I said. “We’re like siblings. Grew up in the I.C. There are only a handful of us.”

"Yeah," Wellington said, "No one else but an Offspring can understand what it is like to be in the I.C."

"Had a hard time making close friends?" I asked.

Wellington nodded. "Whenever I got close to someone, I couldn't. No one could ever understand what we do, and what our relationship was like with our parents."

"No one except a fellow Offspring," I said. "In fact, no one else would or should ever know who *are* the Offsprings in the I.C.," I said.

"Or who is *in* the I.C.," Wellington said.

"So…what are the odds that both of us were coincidentally at Club 85 on that night, locked in the same room with the same fate, numbers man?"

"Almost null," Wellington said.

Then we said it together, "Unless it was the I.C. who arranged the hit on us."

"Fuck," Wellington said.

"Fucked it," I said.

"But who?" Wellington asked.

"I aim to find out," I said. "And why us together? Why take both of us out at the same time?"

Wellington looked at me for a long while and said, "This… just became a game changer."

Chapter 10

Kathryn/Dorothy

I had taken off to Switzerland just as I barely visited Mom at our French chateau. These days, Mom worked from home instead of going into the office. She had been paranoid about catching germs. Said people in her office had been coming down with some kind of illness.

But then again, she saw that as an opportunity to expand our food and now drug supplements empire. That was why she had Dante Black take out her potential competitor Max Millions. Mom wanted to enter into that industry…health and wellness.

Yes, so Max Millions was also a competitor for Clay Black's Black Biotech so it suited Clay to have his own son Dante take out Max Millions. With Max Millions out of the picture and no longer the top of the industry, Black Biotech was next on Mom's hit list. But Clay Black and Dante Black never knew it.

No one in the Inner Circle knew it but Mom and me.

"Go take out Thad Newton," Mom had told me when I was having breakfast with her this morning. “I hear he’s in Switzerland. Became Worth’s new client.”

I almost choke on my espresso. “Like today?” I asked. “I just got here. I was hoping to have some time to get a manicure, go shopping.”

“You can do that any day,” Mom said impatiently.

“Is there a reason you want me to kill Thad Newton? Worth alerted us that he was not Dante Black, as Lion had mistaken. And Newton is the potentially most eligible bachelor in the world so why would I kill him without trying to fuck him first?” I asked. “His portfolio’s incredible. He could potentially be the richest man on Earth.”

“That’ll be great if he beats Bezos,” Mom said. “But that would take him a few years.” She looked over at me and said, “Besides, he isn’t your type. You like the bad boy type, and he's a nerdy geek who would cry like a crybaby if he gets his feelings hurt. Who wants a wimpy man like that? If a man is a wimp, especially if he cries in front of a panel on television like a fucktard whiny crybaby, 100% he must have a limp wimp dick."

"Yeah, definitely not my type, Mom," I said. "But if he's hung like a horse, and he's super rich, that may not matter."

"Whore," Mom said.

"It takes one to know one," I shot back.

"Where did I go wrong?" Mom scoffed.

"When you raised me to be an assassin to do your bidding," I said bitterly.

"I raised you to be in the most elite, most exclusive secret society there will ever be. The Inner Circle. You don't get invited. You don't get added in. You have to be born into it. Respect that," Mom said.

"Respect the rules of the Inner Circle when you're the one putting a hit on members in it? That's rich, Mom, really?"

Mom shrugged. "Don't blame me for watching out for myself," she said. "I may be a hypocrite telling others to do as I say but don't do as I do, but that's because I'm just watching out for numero uno. I'm known to be a witch. I can get away with being a liar without any moral or ethics. Heck, when Dante Black went rogue, I ordered his hit, and his father obliged."

Even I had more sense than Mom was sounding right now. She sounded a bit drunk. And old like a demented bat. Hope I don't ever end up like that when I'm in my 80s. Or maybe Mom was just in her 50s but sound like a 80 year-old.

"What about the other Offsprings?" I asked. "What did Lion and Wizard do to have you put a hit on them?"

"They didn't have to do anything," Mom said. "With Dante Black gone, it occurred to me that taking out the Offsprings was the way to ensure I would never get taken out. Kinda like making sure you remove all barriers to me being forever staying in power. Take out any and all potential rivals, shorten the food supply around the world so we can control people when they're starving, get them hook on our drugs which we conveniently call 'supplements' and 'feel good pills', help fund some lab to create a perpetually mutating illness for the masses that will require them to buy billions of our medicines. See, my plan is working, and soon, we'll control real estate market around the world. I have insider knowledge where to buy because there will be massive building of highways and infrastructure on these lands that I had purposely arranged to own. Then I'll go after the financial sector, play with the fluctuation of stocks and commodities. Farmers will be hurting so that plays into my manipulating food prices. Not to mention other important things people need like minerals, oil, gas, and water."

Wow, I didn't know how big Mom had grown, and how power-hungry she truly was.

"Why all this?" I asked. "We're already doing so well. We're the most elite of the elites."

"Revenge," Mom said. "I want the man who fucking insulted me to pay."

"Who?" I asked. "What did he do?"

“Insulted my pride,” she said. “I wanted him to pay.”

“Who?” I asked again. What man had ticked off Mom like that?

“Clay Black,” she sneered. “He started the Inner Circle, brought us all in. We were all friends. The best in our specialties. Then he went and married some other bitch instead of me.”

“What?” I couldn’t believe my ears. Mom was in love with Dante Black’s father, but he had spurned her love?

“So now I will take over everything he’s ever built, un-do everything he’s ever done, and make the Inner Circle completely mine.”

Mom was demented. Diabolical. Her blue eyes had even darkened into a pupil-less black, like a demon. “You had planned on taking out each of the Founders then.”

Mom smiled a slow but wide smile. “Now you’re thinking like a LaFleur. We may be the top of the Food and Agriculture industry now, but we’ve moved into Clay Black’s sector. With Stan and Scare Crow gone, we’re making our mark in their industry. Entertainment. All that’s left to take over the Inner Circle is Worth’s area which is finance and Lion’s area, which is real estate.”

“Rockefeller’s gone,” I said. “Taken out by Dante, while he was Parker James.”

“And soon, his son Lion will be taken out,” Mom said. “Worth is handling that. He can’t stand mistakes, and since Lion made the mistake of thinking Thad Newton is Dante Black aka Parker James, he will pay for it."

"With his life," I said. I steepled my fingers and leaned back into my 18th century tapestry chair, one of many around our historic chateau. "So why should I go kill Thad Newton?"

"You are dense," Mom said. "Because he owns Black Biotech, which is a rival. Because he also owns a few more companies that will become my rivals."

"Wow, Mom," I laughed, almost maniacally. "You're a bigger bitch than I am. I am impressed."

"Bitch," Mom said.

"It takes one to know one," I shot back.

"Get out of here. Go do your job. Or don't come back," Mom said.

I shoved my cup down on the antique table in front of me so hard, I broke the cup. "Fuck if I ever come back," I said. "I'm out of here." I grabbed my bags and headed out.

Mom didn't even blink or acknowledge me leaving. All she did was gulped down another glass of wine.

Fucking bitch. Fucking tyrant.

As much as I hated her, I was tied to her. For everything. She controlled my inheritance, my future, my life. I couldn't make a move without her telling me to do so. Fuck. If she assigned me to do a hit on Thad Newton, then I have to accept it.

Chapter 11

Thad Newton

Ace and I had changed into business casual attires, ready to finally have dinner at the restaurant next to the hotel. After hearing Lion and Wizard's conversation through the device I had planted on the Wizard, we waited and waited to see what would happen next.

"So?" Ace asked. "Is Wellington, um, the Wizard going to take out Lion?"

“He was supposed to,” I said. “But from the conversation they had about Club 85, it looks like there is a change in the Wizard’s plans.”

“Strange,” Ace said, tapping his earpiece. “I lost him. Not a single sound.”

“He must’ve changed his shirt,” I said.

“So did he or didn’t he?” Ace asked.

“You mean, did he get Lion?” I asked.

“Yes, because if he had, then we’re clear for now. You’re free from being chased by an Offspring out to revenge their founding parent,” Ace smiled.

“No, if Lion’s taken out, that frees up the chance for any of the Offsprings to go after me, not just the one revenging a founder I had taken out."

"So, that nutcase Dorothy, who we thought was Summer, could go after you again? Us? Here in Switzerland?"

"If she knew I was Dante Black," I said. "But word from Worth would have gotten to her and her mother Claire that Thad Newton was not Parker James, hence not Dante."

"Thank God," Ace said. "I wouldn't want a repeat of her visiting us at this hotel. You know. We barely made it out alive."

"I wouldn't be worried about that. She's after Dante, not Thad. So," I clapped my hands together. "We can finally try out that restaurant we've been meaning to."

"A perfect way to end our stay here in Switzerland and head home," Ace said.

"Everything packed?" I asked.

"Ready to go," Ace said. "I even had the hotel pick up our bags to have it delivered to our rental."

"Good," I said, "So we just go have dinner, and we can head straight out to the car."

"Yup," Ace said.

"Perfect," I said, "Let's go. I'm starving."

"Me, too," Ace said. He opened the door and was about to step out when he quickly ducked back in, pushing me away from the door. "Oh no, talk of the nut job."

"Dorothy?" I asked.

Ace nodded. "Heading this way. Deja vue, all over again."

"Are you sure? She must have changed her disguise as Summer Jones into someone else by now," I said.

"Nope, she looks just like Summer," Ace said.

My heart skipped a beat when I heard Summer's name. Maybe it wasn't Dorothy but my Summer. Maybe she was visiting Switzerland on vacation or for business. God, I missed her.

Before I knew it, I opened the door just to make sure Ace wasn't mistaken. I could quickly take a peek.

Too late. As soon as I opened the door, Summer pushed it wide open with her kick.

Then she was on me, jumping on me like a wild cat.

As much as I missed Summer and wanted her to be Summer, I knew she wasn't. She was Dorothy, and it looked like she wanted to kill me.

But why? Did she figure I was Dante Black instead of Thad Newton?

She punched me in the face, but I didn't even tried to block it like I would as Dante or even Parker. I was Thad.

"Oh my God that hurt," I screamed like a woman. "Who are you and what are you doing?"

She jumped off me and stepped back like she had seen a ghost.

I looked behind me and saw Ace. Only he had the platinum silver hair and eyes of Parker James. "Oh my God," she said breathlessly, "It's you."

Ace looked bewildered. He looked over at me and back at Dorothy.

Before we both knew it or even expected, she was all over him, pushing him down on the bed, unzipping his slacks to take his dick into her mouth.

Ace was shocked at first, looking at me helplessly, before he laid his head back and started groaning. I couldn't stop staring. Dorothy, um, looking like my Summer was taking Ace's dick into her luscious mouth and sucking on it hard.

God I missed Summer. I missed her mouth, I missed kissing her there, on her tits, all over her body. I missed eating her pussy. Eating her all out.

Before I knew it, I had stepped up to Summer, um, Dorothy, in a haze and had removed her pants, pulling down her panties at the same time. My mouth was over her folds, licking and sucking, while she sucked Ace's dick.

Chapter 12

Summer/Kathryn/Dorothy

Oh my God, his mouth was on me, and I was loving it. Who knew Thad Newton was so hot in bed.

And Parker James was here with him. As much as I wanted to kill Parker James as a notch on my assassin belt, I wanted to fuck him. I craved being fucked by him. When I pretended to be Summer to him, I had the best sex I've ever had. I loved being with him and how he treated me like I was the most important person to him. I wasn't some whore, some assassin born into a secret society of ruthless assassins. I wasn't my demented senile bat mother's daughter. I was normal and very much loved by this man.

But as Summer Jones.

"Oh fuck," Parker said, "I'm going to explode." I smiled up at him as he closed his eyes and stiffened. Yes, he shot into my mouth, and I swallowed, licking him dry.

I smiled up at him again, and crawled up on the bed, removing my shirt and bra. "I miss you," I cooed. "All of you." I pushed his face down to my breast, rubbing his lips on my erect nipples. "Taste me," I said. "I know you want to, Parker."

He was staring at my breasts so hungrily but didn't make a move.

Meanwhile, Thad's tongue was inside me, fucking me deep while he slid out to lick my folds over and over again.

"Oh God," I whimpered. "Oh so so good."

His tongue circled around my clit teasing it, flicking it, and then sucking on it until I was moaning. "Just enter me now," I screamed out. "Fuck me hard!"

Thad dropped his pants and pulled out an enormous dick. Wow, I was in heaven, in bed with two men with rock hard huge dicks. Thad rubbed his length along my folds, teasing me until I was begging for him to enter me. "Fuck me now, please," I whimpered.

He grinned. Who knew a nerd like him could have the sexiest wicked grin like that. Damn he was hot. Very hot. I wanted his dick like nothing else matter. “Give me your dick now,” I begged.

Thad finally pounded into me, rocking me hard against Parker. He turned me around onto my stomach, lifted me so I was on my knees while he pounded me from behind, thrusting quick and fast. Then slow and deliberate. Oh my God, the man knew how to fuck. Meanwhile, my breasts were rubbing against Parker’s rock hard dick, cradling it in between. I pushed my breasts closer, tightening my grip on his dick, as I moved it in and out between them.

He groaned right as Thad groaned, as he relentlessly thrusted in and out of me. “Oh God,” I closed my eyes shut enjoying the waves of pleasure coursing through me.

I climaxed at the same time Thad pulled out and exploded onto my back.

Parker groaned right as I opened my mouth to take him in deep. I felt his hot liquid pour down my throat as I swallowed. Yes, for the endless pleasure Parker had given me while I stayed with him in his fabulous Malibu house, I'd gladly swallow his load every time.

And Thad, the billionaire wonder tech kid… he was definitely now my type.

Now…about the hit on him and on Parker…

Epilogue

Thad Newton

Ace and I were still relaxed on the same bed as Summer/Dorothy. His face was expressionless as he stared up into the ceiling. Poor Ace, pretending to be Parker, whether for danger or for pleasure, it was getting to him. All that sex, all that running around. Women throwing themselves at him. Yeah, he clearly loved being Parker James, especially right now.

I was already getting up and pulling on my pants. Now that I could see Summer wasn't

Summer, but Dorothy the cold-blooded killer, I wasn't about to be an easy target for her.

But I wasn't about to expose myself as Dante, either.

When she opened her eyes and began getting dressed, I looked sheepish and said, "That was incredible, Miss."

She blinked and said, "You don't know who I am?"

I shook my head, "No, sorry, am I supposed to?"

"But you looked at me as though you recognized me, like you knew me."

"Oh that," I said. "I did recognized you. You're the girl I ordered for some escort service." Then I acted confused. "Or are you?"

"Escort service?" she spat. "Do I look like an escort to you?"

"You do," I said truthfully.

"Well, fuck," she said. "How insulting. I'm more than just an escort." Then she looked over at Ace. "And Parker…what the fuck are you doing here? You know we're all after you."

Ace nodded as Parker. He didn't say anything, careful not to betray his voice. Dorothy would recognize him as Ace if he spoke. After all, she knew Ace when she lived with us at my house in Malibu pretending to be Summer, whom I thought was my girl who ended up with amnesia, having forgotten who I was.

His eyes met mine, and I indicated for him to act quick. Get dressed, get out of bed, and get out. The sexcapade was over, and now Dorothy was back.

And she was in a killer mood. The atmosphere shifted from hot sex to killer tension in zero seconds flat.

Dorothy was watching Ace and me closely. She was naked, but quick as she reached over to grab a gun from a holster that was on the ground. It was hidden underneath her shirt, but was pulled off when she had taken off her top.

I grabbed my gun from *my* holster and pointed it at her, while Ace jumped out of the bed and ran to the door behind me. We had a three-way dance, and the tension was thick.

We stared at each other, watching each other as we waited to see who would make the first move.

Then something went off. A French lullaby melody. I recognize it as Dorothy's.

"Can I get it?" she asked. "Truce for now?"

The phone was closest to me so I picked it up. "Hello?" I spoke into it. I put the phone on speaker.

"Where's Kathryn?" a male voice asked.

"She can't come to the phone right now, but I can take a message," I said.

"Tell her," the man said, "Gerard, her mother's Head of Security, said to get home quickly."

I looked over at Dorothy and watched her while I responded back to the man. “Why?”

“There’s been an emergency,” the man said.

“Yes, but what kind? What happened?” I asked.

“Her mother was just assassinated,” the man said.

Even I was shocked, but Dorothy went red. “Who the fuck did it?” she shouted loud and clear across from the room.

“The security camera caught two men,” the man said. “One large man with long blonde hair and the second was a smaller, thinner man with black hair.”

I knew who he was talking about. So that was where they went, leaving Worth Financials together to go after Claire. The Wizard was working the Lion now.

"Son of a bitch," Dorothy said, getting dressed and clearly pissed off. She walked right pass us to the door, waving us away and no longer interested in taking us out. She grabbed her phone from my hand and said, "I can't believe Wellington and Leo would do such a thing. They took down my mother. Fuck them."

As she pulled her hair into a ponytail, she continued talking to herself. "That might be a good thing, though, because now I have the privilege to take them down." She turned to me and Ace excitedly, "I finally have the privilege as an Offspring to go after and assassinate the ones who took out my mother. My turn," she said.

“Why did someone take your mother down?” I acted dumb again so she would still believe I was only Thad Newton.

“Because dammit, she put a hit on them,” Dorothy said. “Serves her right for doing that.” She looked at me and then Parker. “I’m going to take those two down, revenge my mother, and then I’ll be back for you two. Mark my words.”

She stared hard at both of us before opening the door and leaving, as though nothing happened.

Ace shook his head. “That was unbelievably crazy. She was crazy.”

“It sure was,” I said. “But keep your eyes open still. That may be a ruse. They’re still going to go after us. It’s not safe staying here.”

As though my suspicions were confirmed, my phone rang, and I picked up.

"Mr. Newton," Worth said. "Part of our services to you have been rendered. You asked us to keep your assets safe so we did."

"What do you mean?" I asked.

"Claire LaFleur was after the companies you purchased. She was set to ruin them so she can have a competitive advantage over your industries," Worth explained. "You know she had put a hit on you earlier today. An assassin may be on their way to you, but we intervened. Claire LaFleur would no longer be a problem for you."

"Well…wow, that's just so shocking," I said as Thad, knowing full well that Dorothy was that assassin sent to kill me. "Good job," I said.

"A pleasure," Worth said. "That's Worth Financials way."

"I do feel better going with you guys, then," I said.

"We are happy to have you as a client," Worth said. "But I have to say, Thad, you seemed to be more complicated than you look."

I nodded over the phone.

"Someone spotted you with Parker James earlier. Do you know him personally?" he asked.

"I bought his companies," I said. "I know him that way. Business relationship. Why?"

"Just wondering," Worth said. "If you only knew who he really was, I'd say be very careful around him. He could be an assassin too."

I laughed. “You’re joking aren’t you?”

“No, I’m not. I heard that some assassins don’t ever quit. No matter how much they want to or how they want to get out of it, they can never quit.”

“So if they had a hit on someone that can’t be revoke, it won’t finish until everyone’s in the group is gone?” I asked.

“Everyone,” Worth said.

“Okay, good to know,” I said. “I’ll be on my toes.”

“Good,” Worth said. “Because it ain’t over.”

“Bye!” I said.

"Bye," he said.

I hung up and turned to Ace. "He knows." I said, "He knows I'm Parker James and Dante Black."

"We need to get out of here," Ace said.

"Let's go now," I said. "He's probably making his way here as we speak."

We slipped out the door and hurried down the hallway, but heard some footsteps walking towards our penthouse suite. Ace and I flatten ourselves against the room door until the footsteps walked past us. Then we made our way to the elevator, slipped in and pressed the button to go down.

We were already in our car driving away when we saw Worth himself running out of the hotel lobby searching for us. He was carrying a shotgun, which he pointed at our car, but didn't fire.

As Ace drove as fast as he could, I called my pilot to get my plane ready.

No doubt Worth would be coming right after us especially when he discovered why we were in Switzerland for this long.

We reached my plane in record time and took off. It felt good to be back on safe grounds so to speak.

When we were flying above the hotel at a good height where we can still see the hotel and Worth Financials, I turned to Ace.

"Ready?" I said to Ace.

"Ready," he said.

"Time to put this whole thing to rest. No more Inner Circle. Here's to the last of the Founders…"

With a push of a button in my silver briefcase, we looked down to see the top of the Worth Financials Building blow up.

It was bittersweet as I looked down. Blowing up buildings was my father Clay's signature assassin move. If Worth knew I was Dante, he would also know that was how I would have ended it… something that was a tribute to my father. After all, Clay Black started the Inner Circle.

He would also be the one ending it.

"That was why we were going into the building so often," Ace said. "Not to fix the internet, but to set up the explosives."

"Yes, and to monitor the working hours to make sure we detonated it when no one innocent would be around. Just Worth."

"Smart, Boss," Ace grinned. "Very smart."

I sighed. "Now the real Summer Jones could be safe from the Inner Circle. And I…can become Dante again."

I shook my head. Wait. Worth was right. You can never quit. As an I.C. assassin and an Offspring, you can never stop being who you are. Unless you become someone else completely.

I can never go back to being Dante again. I can't have that life I wanted with Summer. But at least she would be safe from the Inner Circle. Would she?

It was better for me to remain incognito. To be Thad Newton or whoever else I need to morph into. At least she'll be safe. She'll remain alive. I'll make sure she was…even if I have to take down each of the Offsprings too to ensure it.

*****

Dante's story will continue in Book 4 and 5 of The Inner Circle Series.

The Wizard (Inner Circle #4)

Coming 2022

The Lion (The Inner Circle #3)

Dorothy (Inner Circle #5)

Coming
2022

More Books like The Inner Circle

OTHER ROMANTIC THRILLER/SUSPENSE OR REVERSE HAREM BOOK SERIES COMING UP OR JUST RELEASED FROM KAILIN GOW and ROMANCEonTHEgoBOOKS.COM

Hidden Falls High (USA Today Bestselling Spin-off Series of the Loving Summer Series

Hidden Falls High has a new King...

Dante Black, the blackest of the Blacks.

Another home, another new school.

Another target.

Life was supposed to be smooth sailing when you're at the end of your high school year.

Of course it is.

The Lion (The Inner Circle #3)

Especially when you're the one your father relies on to take care of loose ends. And by the time you're 17, you've already earned yourself a reputation amongst the Inner Circle as someone to be feared.

Who am I? I'm the charming Prince, the Golden Boy, the one no one suspects to have no heart.

Until I saw her...my target. The girl I will bring down because she is his crush. Summer.

Who knew crushes could be so cruel?

*****

There is someone new living in the Donovans' old mansion in Hidden Falls, the exclusive enclave in Malibu. He's a senior at the Academy, but he seems older like he's already seen so much in the world. Maybe he has. Maybe he's not of this world.

I thought I had finally found peace at Hidden Falls High...but the nightmare is just beginning...

***Hidden Falls High is a Dark High School Romance

mature YA/New Adult series intended for 17 and up due to language and mature matters. Any sex is consensual.

Cruel Crush
https://www.amazon.com/dp/B081C8VJ3R

Punishing the Princess
https://www.amazon.com/dp/B0847HFDPK

Claiming the Crown
https://www.amazon.com/gp/product/B08996KNGD

The Inner Circle Series (Dante Black's Spin-Off Series)

The Lion (The Inner Circle #3)

I have no qualms about doing the things that I do. I was sent to complete a mission which involved a young woman. She changed me, and that changed everything. Including who and what I am.

I was the Tin Man, and in order for me to live, for her to live, I must take them down. The Inner Circle, aka Oz.

Which means I must take down all the players in Oz, including the Lion, The Scarecrow, Dorothy, and the Wizard.

This is not the Wonderland you read about in fairy tales, but a dark bad place. Before you go, remember to bring an Ax.

**The Inner Circle Series is a Suspenseful Romance, which includes mature themes and scenes. TV-Mature.

The Tin Man (Inner Circle #1) by Kailin Gow
https://www.amazon.com/gp/product/B08HD2QVFD

The Scare Crow (Inner Circle #2) by Kailin Gow
https://www.amazon.com/gp/product/B08KL472YR

The Lion (Inner Circle #3) by Kailin Gow

The Wizard (Inner Circle #4) by Kailin Gow

Dorothy (Inner Circle #5) by Kailin Gow

M.A.G.E. (Magical Academy of Gods and Elementals) Series

The Lion (The Inner Circle #3)

The Princes of Paradise were not what they seemed...
It was supposed to be Paradise...the beautiful island my mother and I moved to for her to start her new job at the luxury resort hotel, The Imperial Cutter Hotel.

It was supposed to be a new start for me at the exclusive elite Academy where I received a scholarship. The beautiful location, new job, a nice new home for us, and prestigious school for me was enough to entice us to the island of Aeros.

But when I met the Cutter Boys, especially Chance, who ruled the island as the son of the owner of The Imperial Cutter Hotel, and whose father started the Academy, all that changed. The most handsome and popular guys on the island, the Cutter Boys were known as the Princes of Paradise.

The Cutter Boys were the most gorgeous and hottest guys I've ever met. Too bad they seem to want me gone but at the same time...can't seem to stop wanting me.

** The M.A.G.E. Magic Academy of Gods and Elementals Series, is a high school/new adult bully romance fantasy series for age 17 and up. All sex is consensual.

Prince of Paradise
https://www.amazon.com/gp/product/B0847HFDPK

Gems of Gods
https://www.amazon.com/Gems-Gods-M-G-Elementals-ebook/dp/B084HHZ8VY

Dance of the Dieties
https://www.amazon.com/gp/product/B084H5GZP4

Magical World Series

A Reverse Harem Paranormal Fantasy Dystopian Romance

Welcome to my world...where there's a war between the those with magic, and those without.

The Lion (The Inner Circle #3)

My name is Kama and I am about to turn 18. In our province, of Arcadia, governed by the Governor, when you become of age and graduate from school, you receive your Life's Plan, which tells you where you would go for college, your profession, where you would live, and even who you will marry.

I'm excited about finding out my Life's Plan because I know I'm going to the same University as my friends, and marrying my long-time boyfriend Liam, the Governor's son. It's almost a sure thing since Liam is the Governor's son.

But something went horribly wrong, and my Life Plan has changed. Everything has changed, including me marrying Liam.

I am also not what I seem. And I'm suddenly able to see the magic around me, including the hot djinn prince and his brother, who seem to desire me as much or more than Liam.

** Magical World Series is a RH Fantasy for Mature

YA/NA due to sexiness and language. If that doesn't bother you then dive right in!

Djinn's Desire
https://www.amazon.com/gp/product/B07XQN3LXH

Djinn's Passion
https://www.amazon.com/gp/product/B07XTHXXLL

Djinn's Destiny
https://www.amazon.com/gp/product/B07XTFBB1R

SOCIETY OF SUPERNATURAL SLEUTHS SERIES

The Lion (The Inner Circle #3)

A Reverse Harem New Adult Paranormal Romance Series

Hot Vampires, Sexy Fae, and a Surprise Supermatural - What is a Human Girl to do with her Society of Hot Supernatural Men?

My name is Scarlet, and I live in strange times. The year is 1890, and Queen Victoria is our Queen. It is a glorious time, where we have steamships, inventions, and exploration.

When I received a mysterious letter from my father's friend, Sherlock Holmes, I am whisked into a world of magic and mystery. A world I never knew exist, until I was able to discover devices from this world. The supernatural world.

I am new to this world, but when I meet a handsome stranger one mysterious night, I am soon initiated into the heart of it. Commissioned to help solve a mystery. Turns out I have some gifts and talents.

Needed for the Society of Supernatural Sleuths.

**Society of Supernatural Sleuths is a 4-book Series, featuring Reverse Harem, mystery, steamy scenes appropriate for mature audiences.

Scarlet's Three
https://www.amazon.com/dp/B07THY596K

Immortal Magic
https://www.amazon.com/dp/B07VMTGW6L

Fae and Fangs
https://www.amazon.com/dp/B07WT8C9HG

Timeless
https://www.amazon.com/dp/B086DCJ3NP

SHADOWLIGHT ACADEMY SERIES

I am not normal. Unlike many high school heroines in fantasy books, I always knew I was not ordinary. Far from it. Since I was two, I have been seeing angels and demons. Given the gift of battle as a warrior, my role as a slayer often interferes with my role as a normal girl. So no, I was never a typical girl who had just found out she was heir to some magical family or something like that. I've been "gifted" practically all my life. So when my ordinary family moved us to San Francisco to a new school where my father teaches, I didn't think much of the school. Shadowlight Academy, the most exclusive and posh prep academy for the super rich. I thought I would be there to slay the evil like an undercover superhero amongst the ordinary. I just didn't think the ordinary would all be extremely unordinary. Especially the three most popular kids in school. Then there's the hot brooding rebel boy who didn't seem to fit in, too. Everyone here has secrets, and I am determined to find out what, before it kills me...the entire Academy and even the world. Okay, I might be dramatizing a bit, but yes, from what I've barely seen...it could be that big. Better get my game gear on and my entire armor on, because this is going to be one epic battle. But who can I trust?The Beautiful Ones, which rule Shadowlight Academy is known to be both beautiful yet wicked. They're fascinated with me as I am of them. But who or what are they really, and why do I feel drawn to them like a fly to a spider? Can I escape their beautiful web before I am trapped forever? Do I want to?

*Shadowlight Academy Series is a NA/high school paranormal academy series for mature teens and up. Expect a tough heroine who can take on anyone and anything, with lots of steam literally and figuratively, and a reverse harem romance.

Shadowlight Academy Series Box Set Part 1 (Books 1 - 3)
https://www.amazon.com/Shadowlight-Academy-Box-Set-Books-ebook/dp/B07ZL711VG

Shadowlight Academy Series Box Set Part 2 (Books 4 - 6)
https://www.amazon.com/Shadowlight-Hunters-Academy-Fantasy-Complete-ebook/dp/B0875R5PY5

BAD BOY ROYALS OF KINGSBURY PREP

RH New Adult/High School Bully Dark Contemporary Romance – HEAT 4 out of 5

Tempest and The Black Envelope (Books 1 and 2) with Bonus and Clue on the Treasure
https://www.amazon.com/dp/B07Z44T1PF

Revenge
https://www.amazon.com/gp/product/B07SQP3HL3

Secret Princess
https://www.amazon.com/dp/B07YLHJ38K

Fallen Royals
https://www.amazon.com/dp/B07XXC625K

Reign of Rebels
https://www.amazon.com/dp/B07XM3FKW6

Complete Series Box Set
https://www.amazon.com/gp/product/B08781CS94

Kingmakers of Kingsbury Series

RH Bully Fantasy Paranormal Shifter Fae Romance – HEAT 4 out of 5

Long before there was an All-Royals Academy called Kingsbury Prep, there was the Kingmaker and her kings.

As Violet Kingsbury, I was born to be a kingmaker. In a time when wars were common and thrones were fought after, the only name that could bring about peace...the only man that could trump the decrees of kings was Kingsbury. The Kingmaker. But when the legendary Kingmaker is disposed, and the time of the Choosing has come, can I, the daughter of The Kingmaker rise to take the place of my father? I am about to find out as the

strongest, most capable, and most legendary princes across the lands come to challenge me for the Choosing including 4 of the most handsome princes who not only wants to win, but to want to win me, too:
Avery
Axel
Reggie
Ollie

Becoming Kingmaker, even as The Kingmaker's daughter, will not be easy in a male world where ladies were supposed to be damsels who needed saving. To become Kingmaker, I will prove to all, especially the princes, that I am here to stay, and will be the one doing the saving. **Kingmakers of Kingsbury Series, is a Reverse Harem Bully Romance with mixed genres elements, action, and mature scenes recommended for age 17 and up.

Kingmaker's Kings (Book 1)
https://www.amazon.com/dp/B082QMNCW4

Kingmaker's Kiss (Book 2)
https://www.amazon.com/gp/product/B084BZYW28

Kingmaker's Kill (Book 3)

https://www.amazon.com/gp/product/B084BT8154

HEARTBREAK FALLS

RH Bully Dark New Adult/High School Romance Mystery – HEAT 4 out of 5

With a name like Heartbreak Falls, one didn't expect to find love at the new town I had moved to courtesy of my new stepfamily aka Mom's new husband and his sons.

Something was up with my new rich stepfather, his

sons, and what happened to their last stepmother. Something was up with the entire town, which my stepfamily seem to run. Along with the school where my stepbrothers reigned as cruel princes. All 3 of them were known as The Heartbreakers. Two were twins and my age, and then there was Tristan, the oldest. Gorgeous but god-awful hateful to me. What was up?
I was about to find out...if I lived long enough.

***Heartbreak Falls is a RH Dark Bully Romance and mystery for 18 and up. It is YA/NA and has themes of bullying and sex. If that's fine with you, then dig in! Bully Me Not is book 1 of 5 and contains a cliffhanger.*

Bully Me Not
https://www.amazon.com/dp/B07XNQV36Q

Break Me Not
https://www.amazon.com/dp/B07XX7HZZZ

Dare Me Not
https://www.amazon.com/dp/B07Z4369V7

Destroy Me Not
https://www.amazon.com/gp/product/B084C143VR

Love Me Not
https://www.amazon.com/gp/product/B084BTRVYN

HOUSE

RH Dark College New Adult Romance – HEAT 5 out of 5

The Lion (The Inner Circle #3)

HOUSE (Book 1 of The House Series) is written as a tv serial. Each book contains a clue to solve the mystery in the end to win a prize of $500 USD!

It was his last will and testament.

For one week, four of us was to live together. Play nice to each other like we used to when we were kids.

Seb, Thomas, Ashford and me.

Three of Mr. Keystone's sons and me, the maid's daughter.

All those years, the three sons bullied and ridiculed me because I was the maid's daughter.

So, why was I back? Why did I cared to be in the same house as those three tormentors?

Because I was in Mr. Keystone's will.

He had always been kind to me, even if his sons weren't, so I could only honor his wishes. And he was like a father to me, and didn't treat me like the maid's daughter. But as soon as I could, I left to go to college. Two years ago. Meanwhile, the boys went their separate ways, too. Estranged from each other.

So why was I here having to live in the same house with his sons for a week?

I don't know, but I'm about to find out, even if it meant my old adolescent feelings for all three of them might surface again. And if being in the mansion we called a house together might jog some memories of the wild nights we've had here.

It's just one week. I could survive that. Or could I?

***House is the first book in The House Series, which is a Reverse Harem Dark Young Adult/New Adult College Romance recommended for age 18+ due to mature themes. This is TV-MA and is high-heat. Also this is Reverse Harem, meaning the FMC will have more than two love interests. Sex is part of the psychological mind games in this series. If this triggers you, then do not read.*

House (The House Series, Book #1)
https://www.amazon.com/gp/product/B0863Z36S5

Haven (The House Series, Book #2)
https://www.amazon.com/gp/product/B087BFJWK5
Habit (The House Series, Book #3)
https://www.amazon.com/gp/product/B087B6MZDM
HEIRS (The House Series, Book #4)
https://www.amazon.com/gp/product/B087BCKS27

The Lion (The Inner Circle #3)

Haunt (The House Series, Book #5)
https://www.amazon.com/gp/product/B087BGL27P
Home (The House Series, Book #6)
https://www.amazon.com/gp/product/B08966PF77

FALLEN FAE ACADEMY

RH Bully Romance Fantasy Paranormal Fae – HEAT 4 out of 5

"At Fallen Fae Academy, the magic will either complete you or kill you."

My name is Harley, as in Harlequin. Plucked from my home

from Las Vegas, NV, and placed into an University on an arts scholarship, suddenly I am the girl the four hottest and most popular boys have decided to "initiate".

This is no ordinary "hazing" ritual, and these boys are no ordinary boys.

This mysterious University looks like any ivy league campus, but it isn't. Step in and you are transported beyond your wildest imagination. I should be ecstatic being here. Except surviving "Initiation" is going to take everything I've got.

Don't let the beauty of the four fae boys fool you. They are as dangerous as they are beautiful. And underneath everything, runs a deep secret. One I need to find out before Initiation kills me.

They think a human is weak. They think I shouldn't be at this university. I'm about to prove them wrong.

**The Fallen Fae Series is a 6-book RH Academy College Bully Romance Series featuring a badass heroine, four deadly, striking fae princes, heart-pounding action, super steamy love scenes, and great romance.

Initiation: Year 1 Fallen Fae Academy Book 1

https://www.amazon.com/Initiation-Year-Academy-Reversed-Paranormal-ebook/dp/B07V9L8LHD

Transformation: Year 2 Fallen Fae Academy Book 2
https://www.amazon.com/dp/B07WWFXVCH

Declaration: Year 3 Fallen Fae Academy Book 3
https://www.amazon.com/gp/product/B07XLMSGDJ

Interruption War Year 3 (Fallen Fae Academy #4)
https://www.amazon.com/dp/B0833JC8YJ

Disruption (Fallen Fae Academy #5)
https://www.amazon.com/dp/B084DB7F1B

Succession (Fallen Fae Academy Book #6)
https://www.amazon.com/dp/B084D4VRCY

Fallen Fae Academy Box Set Part 1 (Books 1 -3)
https://www.amazon.com/gp/product/B08772LQFT

Fallen Fae Academy Box Set Part 2 (Books 4 - 6)
https://www.amazon.com/dp/B08S1C2YZC

<u>CRUEL PRINCES OF WYVERN ALL-BOYS ACADEMY</u>

RH Bully Romance Fantasy Paranormal Shifters) - HEAT 4 out of 5

Enter the Wyvern All-Boys Academy as the Only Girl or Get Killed for Defying the Royal Decree

Diamonds and Dragons (Cruel Princes of Wyvern All-Boys Academy Book 1)
https://www.amazon.com/Diamonds-Dragons-Reverse-Fantasy-All-Boys-ebook/dp/B07SFV1PRH/

Roses and Emeralds (Cruel Princes of Wyvern All-Boys Academy Book 2)
https://www.amazon.com/Roses-Emeralds-Reverse-Fantasy-All-Boys-ebook/dp/B07TS1BKLT/

Silver and Starlight (Cruel Princes of Wyvern All-Boys Academy Book 3)
https://www.amazon.com/dp/B07VXVK2KV

Cruel Princes of Wyvern All-Boys Academy Complete Series Box Set
https://www.amazon.com/gp/product/B086V6ZJKH

About the Author Kailin Gow

From visiting Romania, ALA YALSA Award-winning and Global Million-Selling Author Kailin Gow was asked to write stories about vampires; visiting the Black Forest in Germany and seeing the castles of Europe inspired her to write fantasy; visiting Asia's mystical mountains inspired her to write action adventure and mythological dystopians. From her experience in college as a peer counselor and her volunteer work with women's shelters, she was inspired to write contemporary romance with social issues for women, new adults, young adults, and teens. Having faced adversity, including battling stereotypes and bullying, Kailin Gow has become a well-known speaker and influential figure in media. Her adventurous bold spirit has taken her around the world, where she has ridden on top of elephants through jungles, hand-fed sting rays, studied kung fu from a Shaolin Temple monk, and learned cooking from a celebrity chef. She is a USA Today Bestselling author and has been a #1 Amazon bestselling author over two-hundred times. Her Bitter Frost Series is in development as a TV Series, and her contemporary romance Loving Summer is set to become a feature film. An multi-award-winning filmmaker, director, and actress; Kailin's films have premiered at Cannes, Los Angeles, Rome, England, Paris, Korea, Japan, and even in India's Ministry of Culture.

Compelled to write her first fiction book because of 9/11, Kailin Gow now has over 550 fiction books published under Kailin Gow and various Pen Names in many genres. As a speaker and host, she has hosted international shows at the Pasadena Civic Auditorium, been a celebrity judge at beauty pageants, been a judge for writing contests, and hosted television series. She was featured as an Indie Author Success Story on the homepage of Amazon.com for a month and is also included in Amazon's book called Transformations. She is the first American of Asian Descent to have been featured on Amazon's homepage as an Author Success Story, and the first to have sold over a million books.

Follow Kailin at:

@kailingow
facebook.com/OfficialKailinGow

Kailin Gow's Reverse Harem Reader Group
(Kailin Gow's Kingdom)
https://www.facebook.com/groups/927167070954766/

Kailin Gow RH Newsletter Sign Up

http://madmimi.com/signups/5d7494ecee0a46feaa5c7a60f8f152f1/join

Bookbub
https://www.bookbub.com/authors/kailin-gow

Amazon Author Page
https://www.amazon.com/Kailin-Gow/e/B002BMAEH4

Twitter
https://twitter.com/kailingow

Instagram

https://www.instagram.com/kailingow

YouTube

https://www.youtube.com/user/Sparklesoup/videos

www.ingramcontent.com/pod-product-compliance
Ingram Content Group UK Ltd.
Pitfield, Milton Keynes, MK11 3LW, UK
UKHW041828200726
13854UKWH00002BA/885

9 798450 891262